Little Brother of War

Gary Robinson

D1052044

7th Generation
Summertown, Tennessee

7th Generation, an imprint of
Book Publishing Company
PO Box 99, Summertown, TN 38483
888-260-8458
bookpubco.com
nativevoicesbooks.com

ISBN: 978-1-939053-02-2

18 17 16 15 14 13   1 2 3 4 5 6 7 8 9

Printed in the United States

Library of Congress Cataloging-in-Publication Data
Robinson, Gary, 1950-
   Little Brother of War / Gary Robinson.
      pages cm
   ISBN 978-1-939053-02-2 (pbk.) -- ISBN 978-1-939053-88-6 (e-book)
   [1. Individuality--Fiction. 2. Ball games--Fiction. 3. Choctaw Indians--
   Fiction. 4. Indians of North America--Mississippi--Fiction. 5. Family life--
   Mississippi--Fiction. 6. Brothers--Fiction. 7. Mississippi--Fiction.] I. Title.
   PZ7.R56577Lit 2013
   [Fic]--dc23

                                    2013013182

Book Publishing Company is a member of Green Press Initiative. We chose to print this title on paper with 100% postconsumer recycled content, processed without chlorine, which saved the following natural resources:
• 15 trees
• 470 pounds of solid waste
• 7,023 gallons of water
• 1,294 pounds of greenhouse gases
• 6 million BTU of energy

green press INITIATIVE

For more information on Green Press Initiative, visit www.greenpressinitiative.org. Environmental impact estimates were made using the Environmental Defense Fund Paper Calculator. For more information visit www.papercalculator.org.

Contents

Author's Note

The ancient game of Choctaw stickball that is the subject of this story is but one form of this game known and played by many tribes in North America. The tribes of the Iroquois Confederacy in regions of New York and southern Canada played the game with only one stick. French priests who visited those tribes in the 1600s were the first Europeans to observe the sport. The priests called it *lacrosse* in their writings, and a modified form of the game became popular in Europe. Different tribes have different names for this game, but some northern and southern tribes called it "Little Brother of War" or "Little War" in their tribal language. Today, lacrosse is enjoying increased popularity and is played by high school, college, and professional teams all across America.

Little Brother of War

of War

Gary Robinson

Chapter 1
The First Day

My big brother was good at everything he did. And as far back as I can remember, Mom and Dad always compared me to him.

"Why can't you be more like Jack?" Dad would say. Or, "It's time to get it together, Randy. Your brother had already made the football team at your age."

Jack was a football hero in both middle school and high school. Everyone worshipped him. Especially my dad. But no matter how hard I tried, I just couldn't follow in his footsteps. I could only live in his shadow.

When he graduated, Jack joined the Army and was shipped off to the war in Iraq. My parents acted like the most important person in the world had left them.

Soon after that, Jack became a war hero. He captured a group of enemy soldiers who were about to launch an attack against his platoon. He saved their lives.

The whole state was proud of him then. The Mississippi Choctaw tribal newspaper announced the news to everyone in the tribe. The TV news broadcast his achievement to everyone in Mississippi.

And sure, I was proud of him too. But how was I ever going to follow in those footsteps? A football hero and a war hero!

Then, when he was killed in a helicopter crash over there, my parents acted like their only son had died.

Of course, it was a terrible thing. We were all sad about it. I cried for days. But I was still alive. My parents' other son was still here. But they lost interest in everything. Everything but the memory of Jack.

And what was I supposed to do after my brother died? My life had been spent trying to live up to his successes. Trying to make my parents as proud of me as they were of him. But I just wasn't good enough.

That's the reality I faced as I dressed for my first day at Choctaw Central High School. The school where my brother had been named Most Valuable Player on the football team.

It was also the school where my father had played baseball when he was a teenager. He'd been their star pitcher in those days.

The only award I'd won so far was third place in the ninth grade spelling bee. Whoop-de-do.

I was nervous as I sat down at the breakfast table. Dad was sure to say something about what a big deal it was. Going off to high school. Carrying on the family sports tradition. Following in my brother's footsteps.

Mom was cooking at the kitchen stove. During the school year, she made breakfast every morning for Dad and me. Then she'd drive up the road to her job at the Red Water Elementary School.

As usual, Dad was reading the newspaper.

"Ready for the big day?" he asked. "Ready for high school?" He didn't look up from the paper.

"I guess." I shrugged my shoulders.

"Did you get all your school supplies?" This time he looked at me.

"No," I replied. "Mom didn't have time to take me." I braced myself to get yelled at. That's what usually happened.

Instead, he looked at Mom for a moment with disapproval. Then Dad picked up a sack that sat on the floor beside his chair.

"Here," he said as he handed me the sack and looked back at his newspaper.

It was a sack from the Fall-Mart store. That's where Dad had worked since he had gotten laid off from the tribal casino.

Inside the sack was a collection of the school supplies I needed.

"Wow, Dad," I exclaimed. "This is a surprise."

"They promoted me to stock manager," he said. "I get a great employee discount now."

Mom put down a plate of food in front of me that looked delicious. It was her special scrambled eggs and grits. I practically inhaled it.

As I finished eating, Dad left the room to get ready for work. When we could hear him brushing his teeth in the bathroom, Mom sat down beside me.

"Randy, your father couldn't go to college because of his grades," she said. "He doesn't have a big, important job. And he's always wanted more for you boys."

"Yeah, I know."

"That's why he always pushed for you and Jack to do well," she continued. "So you'd have a better life than he's been able to provide."

"Well, that's not what I hear," I said. Suddenly I felt angry. "All I hear is how I'm not good enough. How I don't measure up to Jack!"

I left the kitchen carrying the sack of school supplies. I went into my room to find my backpack. Mom followed me.

"That's what I'm trying to explain," she said. "Since your dad didn't do well in the classroom, sports became the only way for him to excel. Sports are important to him."

"Yeah, that message has come through loud and strong," I said with an edge in my voice. "Both of you have made that clear."

I threw the new school supplies in my backpack and headed for the front door. Again my mother followed.

"Randy, please listen!"

I stopped with my hand on the doorknob. Turning back to Mom, I waited to hear what she had to say.

"Your father and I just want you to do your best. That's all. That's all anyone can do, really."

"Well, you'd better get used to third place, then, because that seems to be the best I can do!"

I ran out the door before Mom could say anything else. I'd had enough of that conversation. What a way to begin my first day of high school.

I walked down our street to wait for my ride to school. We lived in a neighborhood of little brick Indian houses in the Red Water community. Some government agency had built them for Choctaw families before I was born.

To get one of these homes, Mom and Dad had to help with the construction. That was part of the deal that made it easier for Indian families to buy their own homes and make lower house payments.

My ride showed up just as I reached the corner. Oddly enough, my so-called girlfriend and her mother would be taking me to school this year.

"Hello, Randy," Mrs. Jimmie said from the driver's seat.

"Hi, Randy," Jennifer said in a sweet voice from the front passenger seat.

I jumped in the back, and we sped off down the road. Jennifer had sort of become my girlfriend last summer, by accident.

Her family lived on the next street over from our family. One day, while we were exploring the woods behind my house, she suddenly kissed me. Boy, was I surprised.

Ever since then she said I was her boyfriend. I didn't mind. She was pretty. I didn't know exactly what a boyfriend was supposed to do, but I figured I'd find out.

Anyway, Mrs. Jimmie had offered to give me a ride to school this year since she worked at the Choctaw tribal office near the school. Riding the bus would take an hour. It would take Mrs. Jimmie less than half an hour to go the twenty miles to Pearl River.

Chapter 2
Big Shoes

Jennifer and I walked into school together. A big sign with Choctaw designs around the edge greeted us in the hallway. "Welcome New Students," it read. Everyone who went to this school was Choctaw.

"I hope we have lunch at the same time," Jennifer said and gave me a quick peck on the cheek. "Good luck finding your homeroom," she added as she walked down the hall.

I took the paper out of my backpack that listed all my classes. As I read the room number for the first one, a man's voice startled me.

"You're Randy Cheska, right?" the man said. I looked up to see a tall African American man wearing a suit. He held his hand out to me, so I shook it.

Next to him stood a stocky Indian man wearing sweats. The words "Central Choctaw Warriors" were printed on his shirt. A strap hung from around his neck with a whistle on the end of it.

"I'm principal Bill Gilroy," the man in the suit said. "And this is Coach Boles. He's in charge of our football program." Principal Gilroy kept shaking my hand. Finally he stopped.

"Hi," is all I said. The school principal had found me as soon as I set foot in the new school. What was going on? Was I already in trouble?

"We wanted to personally welcome you to Choctaw Central High School," Coach Boles said. "And there's something we want you to see."

They led me down the hall to a big glass case. Inside the case was a large, shiny trophy with a little football player on top. A few smaller trophies stood near it.

"Do you know what that is?" the principal asked.

"A football trophy?" I guessed.

"Not just *any* football trophy," the coach replied. "That's the trophy your brother won for us his senior year. We won the all-state championship thanks to him."

He pointed to a picture that was stuck on the wall with big tacks. It was a shot of Jack in his football uniform. Next to it was a newspaper article about the team's win that year.

Uh-oh, I thought. I didn't know if I liked where this was going.

"And take a look over here," Coach Boles said. He led the way to the next glass case. There was another trophy. It looked older and less shiny. This one had a little baseball player on it. There were some faded old newspaper pages tacked up beside it.

"Can you guess whose trophy this is?" Principal Gilroy asked.

"My dad's?" I guessed. Now I knew for sure I didn't like where this was going.

"That's right!" both men said at the same time.

"Son, you come from strong sports blood," the coach said. "And we want to do everything we can to help you step into the big shoes your father and brother wore."

What were they talking about? They still had my dad's shoes? And they wanted me to wear them?

"I don't understand," I said.

Coach Boles put his hands on my shoulders and turned me toward him.

"What we're saying, Randy, is that we're excited about you being here," he said. "And we want to help you get started in whatever team sport you want to play. We know you want to make your brother and your father proud."

"Oh, I see," I said. "You're after another state championship."

"Now you've got the picture," the principal said. "Get settled in here at school for a few days. Then we'll get together and talk sports. Fair enough?"

"Yeah, sure," I muttered. Then I thought of my class. I was probably late for it. I held up the paper in my hand.

"Here, let me show you where that classroom is," Principal Gilroy said. "I'll let the teacher know you're not late."

He walked me down a couple of long halls and introduced me to my homeroom teacher, Mrs. Sanford.

"This is the Cheska boy," the principal told the teacher. "We've got big plans for him this year." Then he whispered, "I want you to take special care of him."

"Will do, Mr. Gilroy," the teacher said as the principal left.

Mrs. Sanford led me to an empty seat at the front of the class.

"You can sit right here," she said. "That way I can keep an eye on you for Mr. Gilroy."

That's just great, I thought. I didn't want special attention. I just wanted to blend in with everyone else.

I looked at the students around me as I sat down in my chair. I didn't like what I saw in their faces. Attitude. I could tell they already saw me as the teacher's pet.

This definitely wasn't a good start to my high school career. How was I going to break the news to all of them that I wasn't any good at sports? That the athletic blood didn't flow in my veins.

When I got home that afternoon, Mom asked me how my first day of high school had gone.

"I don't want to talk about it," I said as I made a beeline for my room. Mom didn't follow me in. Thankfully, she left me alone in my misery.

I turned on music and started playing my Temple Raider computer game as I lay on the bed. But it wasn't long before Mom knocked on my door.

"I have afternoon snacks," she said in a cheery voice.

I was pretty sure there would be a price for accepting those snacks. Not in money, but in parental advice I didn't really want. But I knew Mom meant well.

"Bring 'em on in," I replied with a sigh.

Mom came in carrying a tray of mini pizza rolls and a soda. She set them down on a corner of my desk. I got up, popped a pizza roll in my mouth, and followed it with a gulp of soda.

"So did anything interesting happen at school today?" she asked. So that's what this was about.

"Yeah," I answered. "I was ambushed by the principal and the football coach first thing. It's bad enough to get this pressure at home. Now I'm going to face it every day at school!" I grabbed another pizza roll and started pacing.

"That's what I want to talk to you about." Mom popped a pizza roll in her mouth. I continued to pace as I waited for her speech to begin.

"I get that football and baseball are not your thing," she said. That stopped me in my tracks.

"You do?" I said with surprise in my voice. "When did that happen?'

"I was trying to tell you that this morning, but it came out all wrong."

"What about Dad?" I asked. "What's he say about this?"

"I haven't talked to him about it yet," Mom admitted. I started pacing again. Having Mom on my side is one thing. Convincing Dad is something else entirely.

"But I'm going to start working on him, little by little," she added as she stood to leave. "Meanwhile, it would be good if you figured out something you really want to try instead. Something new you could learn how to do and practice at. You know, something you care about."

I'd have to give that some thought. I knew I'd mostly be busy just trying to get by with schoolwork. Taking on something more could be too much to handle.

"Okay," I said finally. "I'll think about it."

"Good," Mom said as she headed for the door with a smile.

There was hope that I wouldn't have to try to wear my dad's and brother's big shoes after all.

Chapter 3
The Second Day

As I tried to fall asleep that night, the talk with my mother and everything that had happened at school swirled around in my head. On top of that, I also remembered it had been about a year since Jack had died. All that stuff mashed together in my mind made it hard to go to sleep.

My weird first day of high school was followed by a weird night of sleep. What was so weird? Jack appeared to me in a dream. I usually don't remember my dreams. But I remembered this one.

In the dream I was standing on a rocky hilltop. It didn't look like anything where we lived. Dragging his rifle behind him, Jack climbed up the hill toward me. He was wearing his combat uniform. When he got to the top of the hill, he saw me and rushed over to me.

"I've been looking for you," he said. "I need to tell you something, little brother."

I tried to speak, but couldn't.

"Don't follow in my footsteps," he said. "My path led to war. You can be a different kind of warrior."

Again I tried to speak. "But Dad and the coach—" I said. That was all that came out of my mouth.

"Don't worry about them," he said. "Tomorrow is the first day of the rest of your life. Be your own man."

He looked away, as if he heard something, and nodded.

"I've got to go," he said. He looked back at me. "Remember this dream, little brother. Everything's going to be all right eventually. You'll see."

With that, he faded away, and I woke up.

The next morning, as I dressed for my second day of high school, things seemed somehow different. It felt as though a cloud had lifted. A fog had vanished. The shadow I had been living under had disappeared.

Or was I just imagining this? I certainly couldn't tell Mom and Dad about the dream. They'd think I had gone nuts. Or they'd tell me it had nothing to do with reality.

Nothing was really different at the breakfast table. Dad was still Dad. Mom was still hopeful. I could tell by the little smile she had.

The rest of the week was pretty much the same as usual. I don't know what I expected. Jack did say things would be all right "eventually." Not right away.

I settled into the new school routine. Mrs. Jimmie took me and Jennifer to school in the morning. Then she drove us home again in the afternoon. Sometimes Jennifer rode in the front with her mom. Other times she rode in the back seat with me. It was all okay.

At breakfast Saturday morning, Mom said, "The Choctaw Cultural Fair is being held at the Red Water Community Center today. Do you want to go with me?"

"Nah, not really."

"Jennifer might be there," Mom said.

"That's okay," I replied. "I see her every day."

"They're serving Indian tacos for lunch."

"Well, that's different," I said. "I guess I don't have anything better to do."

"We'll leave about ten o'clock."

"Just so we don't stay too long, okay?" I said as I got up from the table.

"Okay," Mom agreed.

At ten o'clock we drove the few short miles to the community center. A banner over the front door announced "Choctaw Cultural Fair" and had Choctaw designs all over the background.

A few Choctaw people were going inside. I recognized some of them from different tribal events and last year's Choctaw Fair held in July. There were kids, parents, and grandparents. Traditional Choctaw songs played over a loudspeaker.

"I'm going to watch the elder women making Choctaw dolls," Mom said. "What are you going to do?"

"I'll just look around and see what's here," I replied. "How long do you want to stay?"

"A couple of hours, at least," Mom said as she headed for the doll room. "We'll have lunch about noon. They're serving those Indian tacos in the cafeteria. See you then."

She walked on down the hall, leaving me on my own. What was I going to do to kill two hours? There probably wasn't much here I was interested in seeing.

I wandered to the gathering room where the music was coming from. Couples dressed in traditional Choctaw clothes were dancing. I think it was the Snake Dance. I had seen that a few times before. Holding hands, the dancers formed a long line that coiled and uncoiled like a snake.

A girl at the end of the line of dancers saw me standing near the door. She waved for me to come join in the line. No thanks. That was my signal to leave before I got sucked in.

I didn't find anything really interesting in the front part of the building. So I wandered down the hall and toward the back door.

An elderly Choctaw man sat at a table near the door. He wore a pair of striped overalls. He was hard at work carving a piece of wood. When I got up near him I saw that he was making a stick for Choctaw stickball.

Of course, I'd seen people playing Choctaw stickball before. Lots of times. The game had been around for centuries. But I'd never seen anyone making the sticks. I moved in closer to get a better look.

"Do you play?" the man asked me.

"No, just watch," I answered. "Those look hard to make."

"Not when you've been making them as long as I have," he said. "My name's Albert Isaac." He put out his hand and I shook it.

"I'm Randy Cheska."

"Pleased to meet you, Randy." He picked up a pair of sticks sitting on the chair beside him. He held them out to me. "Why don't you see how these feel in your hands?"

I took the sticks from him. The wood had been sanded smooth. It was a light tan color. "What kind of wood is this, Mr. Isaac?" I asked.

"Call me Albert," he said. "Hickory. I only use hickory. It's the best wood for making ball sticks." He continued carving the stick he held.

"Do you know the Choctaw word for this game?" Albert asked after a moment.

"No. If I did, I forgot," I admitted.

"*Toli*," he said. "And the stick is called *kapoca*."

I looked closer at the curved ends of the sticks. Each had several strands of leather stretched across the rounded opening. It made a little net. That's where you catch the ball.

As I turned the sticks in my hand, I saw that there was a letter stamped into the bottom of each stick. There was an *A* on one and an *I* on the other.

"What are these letters doing on the bottom of the sticks?" I asked.

"That's my trademark," he answered. "*A* for Albert. *I* for Isaac. I stamp that into every pair of sticks I make."

Next he handed me one of the small leather balls he'd made. It was a little bigger than a golf ball, but softer.

"The Choctaw word for this ball is *towa*," Albert said. "Let me hear you say all three Choctaw words I just taught you."

"Toli, kapoca, towa," I repeated. "Is that right?"

"Very good!"

Just then I heard people outside hollering. They were excited about something. I looked out and saw there was a group of guys playing a ball game, I mean toli, in the field behind the community center.

"I have an idea," Albert said. "Why don't you take that pair of kapoca and try them out for me? I like to make sure all my sticks work properly before I give them to the person who ordered them."

"Oh no, I couldn't," I protested. "What if I break one?"

"That would mean that I didn't make this pair strong enough."

"But I don't know the rules of the game, or even how to catch the ball, er, towa," I said.

"The rules are easy," Albert said. "You can't touch the towa with your hands. You have to use the two kapoca to pick up and throw the ball toward the goal. You can hit other players with your body to block them. But you must never try to hit anyone with your kapoca. That's it."

"Okay, I guess I'll give it a shot."

"Good luck," Albert offered. "Have fun."

Chapter 4
Play Ball

I moved out the back door and toward the field. It looked like about twenty players were in the game. Ten on a team. Another ten or fifteen people watched from the sidelines.

At either end of the field stood a wooden goalpost. Each post was about ten or twelve feet tall.

The two teams lined up facing each other near the center of the field. One team wore red armbands. The other wore blue ones.

Between the facing rows, at the center of the field, stood a player from each team. There was a man in between them holding the towa. When he thought both teams were ready, he threw the towa up in the air and backed out of the way.

The two center players jumped up trying to catch the ball in their ball sticks. They missed and the ball hit the ground. Immediately a few players from each team rushed toward the towa. Their sticks were stretched out in front of them.

They crowded together trying to pick up the ball. The group became a large moving mass as they circled the ball. Their kapoca clattered against one another. Each group tried to capture the ball.

Finally one player grasped the towa with both sticks and pulled out of the crowd. He flung the ball to another teammate who stood closer to the opponent's goal. A player from the opposing team got hold of the ball instead.

Cupping the ball with his sticks, he shot the towa in the opposite direction. And the play of the game continued like that. Players whooped and hollered in their excitement. Spectators yelled out the names of players to encourage them. It was all very exciting.

The man who had thrown up the ball noticed me watching from the sidelines. He came over.

"I see you have a pair of kapoca," he said. "Do you want to play?"

"I guess so," I answered. "I've never played before."

"That's okay. We've got to get someone to go in on the other side so the teams won't be uneven."

He signaled to another boy who stood nearby. The boy grabbed a pair of sticks that lay on the ground and ran over to us.

"James, this is—what's your name?" the man said.

"Randy," I answered.

"This is my son, James, and I'm Carl Tubby."

We shook hands all around.

"James, Randy wants to play. He's new to the game, so go easy on him."

"Yes, sir," James replied. "We can jump in after the next point."

We focused back on the game just as the ball was tossed from a player on the left end of the field. The towa whizzed through the air.

Surprisingly, his teammate caught it between the cupped ends of his sticks.

Immediately he turned toward the upright goalpost at the end of the field. He heaved the ball at top speed and it hit the post. His team screamed a victory yell. So did a few spectators.

Others moaned and complained. I guessed they were supporting the other team.

"Let's go line up," James said and ran onto the field.

The players lined up as they had done before. James joined one line of players and pointed to the other line across from him.

"Stand over there." He pointed to a gap in the other line of players.

Meanwhile, I saw Mr. Tubby talking to the captain of my team. He pointed at me and the captain nodded his head. The captain walked over carrying a red armband.

"Welcome to the team. Put this on." He handed me the armband. "Just stay mostly in the middle of the field. If the ball comes near you, join the battle to get it. Toss it on to one of our players closer to the goal."

"I'll try," I said as the captain walked back to his position.

"Watch your back," James called over to me. "I wouldn't want you to get hurt your first time."

"Thanks. Wish me luck."

"No way. I want my team to win."

Just then the referee threw up the ball and the next round began. I panicked. What was I doing? I was no good at sports! Too late. The ball was in play and so was I!

The action moved up and down the field really fast. First one team had possession of the towa, then the other. The players ran back and forth and tossed the ball back and forth many times before anyone made a goal.

The whole thing was exciting and exhausting at the same time. I can't remember when I'd had so much fun. It turned out that you didn't have to be a pro to play this game. You just had to do your best. The more I played, the more I got the hang of it.

After each point was scored, the teams gathered on the side of the field for a few minutes to rest and drink water. Each team had its own bucket of water to drink from. A ladle that hung from the side of the bucket was used to get a drink.

As I waited for my turn with the ladle, I saw that the score was eight to six, our favor. Wow, I was on a winning team! How unusual.

The captain, whose name was Travis, stood nearby as I sipped a scoop of water.

"You're not doing bad for a beginner," he said. "We'll be playing again next Saturday, if you want to join us."

Just then I heard my mother's voice call from over near the back door of the community center.

"Randy?" she shouted. "Are you out here?"

"Yeah, Mom," I answered. "I'm over here." I waved so she could see me in the middle of all the players. She walked over.

"What are you doing?" she asked, and then looked at me harder. "What happened to you? You've got cuts and scrapes all over you. Are you all right?"

I looked down at my legs and arms. There were little cuts here and there. My elbow was scraped. One knee was bruised.

"Oh, that," I said. "I hadn't really noticed. I guess those happened while I was playing."

"Well, it's way past noon," she said. "We were supposed to have lunch together."

"I'm sorry," I said. "I lost track of the time. We only need two more points to win the game. Can I stay a little while longer?"

Mom looked a little surprised and worried. "I guess so, if you want to," she answered. "Aren't you getting hungry?"

"Yeah, but I can wait to eat." The referee called for the players to gather for the next round.

"I've got to go," I told her as I walked back onto the field. "But you can't watch. That'll make me nervous."

"Okay, I'll go back inside," she called.

I ran to get my place in line. I didn't want to miss a single minute of the game.

Chapter 5
A Mystery

We played on for another hour. When the game ended we had lost by only one point. The final score was ten to nine.

Our team gathered on the sidelines to drink some water and talk.

"Guys, that was a hard-fought game," our team captain said. "The score was close and could've gone either way. I'm especially proud of how our new player, Randy, handled himself." What? Did I hear that right? Who was he talking about?

He looked at me. "You have some natural skills, young man. I don't think you even realize it."

He started clapping and everyone on the team did, too. I blushed.

"Okay, we're done here," he finished up. "Be back here next Saturday at ten o'clock if you want to play again."

The guys gathered their gear and the group broke up. The team captain walked with me as I headed back to the community center.

"My name's Charley Rabbit, by the way," he said. We shook hands. "You're included in that invitation to play next week, you know."

"I don't even have my own sticks," I answered. "I just borrowed these from Mr. Isaac."

"Who's Mr. Isaac?"

"The old man inside the center," I said just as we arrived at the back door. "He was in the back hallway here making sticks."

Charley opened the back door and we went inside. I looked for Albert, but there was no sign of him.

"He was sitting at a table right here making ball sticks," I said. I was confused. Where could he have gone? How was I going to return the sticks to him?

I noticed a janitor sweeping the hall. I approached him.

"Excuse me. Do you know what happened to Mr. Isaac, the elderly man who was here before?"

"I'm sorry but I didn't see anybody," the janitor replied. "I got here about an hour ago and there wasn't anyone in this hall." He went on with his sweeping.

"I guess you've got yourself a brand new pair of kapoca," Charley said. "At least for the time being."

Just then Mom came around the corner and into the hall.

"There you are," she said. "And are you ever sweaty and dirty. It's the shower for you when we get home."

"Can we eat first? I'm starved," I said. "This is Charley. He's the captain of a toli team." I saw Mom's puzzled look. "Stickball," I explained.

"Oh, right," she said. "Nice to meet you." Then to me, "Give the man back his sticks so we can go."

"Those are Randy's sticks now," Charley told Mom. "Maybe I'll see you next week," he said to me as he walked away.

Now it was Mom's turn to be confused.

"What's going—?"

I interrupted. "Can we go eat? I really am starving."

As we ate our Indian tacos, I told Mom all about Albert Isaac and the sticks he'd loaned me. I also told her about Carl and James Tubby and the game we'd just played.

I think Mom found it all surprising and a little puzzling. She just listened to me. She didn't ask questions or say anything. But I could see the gears in her mind turning. She seemed to be taking it all in and thinking about it. But what would Mom do with this information?

"Well, when we see this Mr. Isaac again you'll have to give him his sticks back," she said finally.

"Of course," I said.

When we got home, Dad was watching a college football game on TV. The University of Mississippi was playing the University of Tennessee. In his lap sat the family photo album with all of Jack's football and Army pictures. Dad's eyes were red. I think he'd been crying.

"Jack could've been playing college football right now if he hadn't joined the Army," he said. "I never really understood why he wanted to be a soldier."

I saw Mom get a worried look on her face. She patted me on the arm.

"Randy, you go on and take a shower," she said. "I'm going to talk to Dad for a little bit."

I went for the shower. I'd seen Dad get like this more and more since Jack died. He starts thinking about what could've been. What if Jack had gone to college instead of enlisting in the Army? What if Mom and Dad had saved enough money for Jack to go to college? What if Jack were still alive?

It's the kind of thing you think about when life doesn't go as you planned. What if, what if, what if.

After the shower I went into my room. I picked up the ball sticks that were resting on the bed. I decided to do some digging.

I turned on my laptop and clicked on my Internet browser. When the tribe installed cable TV in our neighborhood, they also included Internet access. I navigated to the Wikipedia site and typed "Mississippi Choctaw Stickball" in the search field.

A page came up that had several paragraphs on the game, along with an old picture. I read about the history of the game and saw that other tribes in our area of the country also played the game. This included the Cherokee and Creek tribes.

Then I clicked on a link on that page that said "lacrosse." That took me to another Wikipedia page about this modern game. It said that some of the tribes in the northern part of the United States play stickball with one stick. That game has a longer stick with a bigger net. French explorers saw Native people playing this game more than two hundred years ago and brought it back to

France. From there it became the worldwide sport known as lacrosse.

After a short while, Mom came into my room to talk.

"Randy, I'm sure you're a little curious about what's going on with your father."

"Yeah, I guess," I said.

"His mind is sort of stuck. He can't move on with life. And he gets these headaches. They sort of flash through his brain. He can't see for a minute or two," Mom explained. Her voice was filled with worry.

"Those things sound serious," I replied.

"I've finally talked him into seeing a doctor, a specialist, about it. So he can get help."

"What kind of doctor?" I asked.

"Two different doctors, actually. First, a brain specialist to see about the headaches. The other one is a doctor for the mind. He's called a psychologist."

"I've heard of that," I said. "Does that mean Dad's crazy?"

Mom laughed. "No, not at all," she said. "Lots of people have trouble with something that's happened in their lives. Maybe they get depressed. Or have trouble controlling their emotions. Things like that."

"Okay. I get it," I replied.

"There may be some medicine your father can take that will help him," Mom said. "We won't know until he sees the doctors in a few days. In the meantime, we need to try to be patient with him. Okay?"

"Sure. No problem."

I needed to think about all this, so I told Mom I was going for a walk in the woods behind our house. The outdoors always had a way of clearing my head and making me feel better.

I followed the path I always took. I had no idea who or what created the path. It was just there, winding its way through the trees. These woods were filled with jackrabbits, squirrels, and all types of birds. They scattered and hid when people showed up. Too bad.

I kind of wished I knew more about the plants and animals that lived there. When I was little, my grandma would tell me that we Choctaws had a use for every plant in the forest. And we knew every animal that walked on the land. But she got really sick. She asked for certain herbs from the woods that could heal her, but nobody knew what they were. If someone in our family had known what those plants looked like, she might have lived.

Thinking about Grandma made me remember Mr. Isaac. Who was that old man and where did he disappear to? I had heard some strange stories about old Indian beliefs. Things you couldn't explain. Some people called them mysteries.

Chapter 6
Opportunity Knocks

The next Monday I was back at school and in my homeroom class. Mrs. Sanford was telling us what she expected us to do the coming week.

The classroom door opened and in walked Principal Gilroy. Uh-oh, I thought. They've come for me.

"Sorry to interrupt," Mr. Gilroy said. "I need to borrow the Cheska boy for a few minutes."

Mrs. Sanford really had no choice. She nodded and the principal signaled to me. "Coach Boles and I would like to have a few words with you," he said. I followed him out the door.

The coach was already waiting in Mr. Gilroy's office.

"Randy, so good to see you," the coach said. "Have you been thinking about which sport you want to play for us?"

"Can I see a list of sports you have available?" I asked. "I haven't had time to think about it. I've really been busy getting used to high school."

"Oh," Mr. Gilroy said. "Coach, give Randy our list of sports. He needs to be fully informed before he can make his decision."

The coach left for a few minutes and came back with a computer printout from the school athletics department. I took the paper from him and gave it a quick look. There were seven team sports on the list. Of course the big three were there: football, basketball, and baseball. But also softball, soccer, track, and even golf. No stickball.

"I'll take this list with me so I can think it over," I said. "Give me a week."

"All right," the coach replied. He wasn't too happy about it. "A week. But no longer. We need to get you started with workouts and practices right away."

"Sure," I said and left as quickly as I could. I needed to stall for time. I had to think of a way to tell them I wasn't interested in any of the sports on their list. I wasn't any good at them either. And I had to think about what I was going to tell Dad.

I couldn't talk to Jennifer or her mom about any of this. They might accidentally spill the beans to someone. And that someone might blab to the coach or my dad.

The following Saturday Dad had to work. That made it easy for Mom to take me back to the Red Water Community Center for another game of toli. And Dad wouldn't have to know about it yet.

Charley said he was happy to see me back again for another game. Mom agreed to come and pick me up in about three hours.

James and Mr. Tubby were there, too, all set to go.

"Ready for another beating?" James asked as a taunt.

"You only beat us by one point," I said sharply. "That's not a beating. That's just squeaking by."

James smiled. I knew this was part of the fun of it all. Teasing each other.

"We'll just see who's going to beat who this time," I said with a smile of my own.

Mr. Tubby called the teams to begin the game. Everything got real serious real fast. He threw the towa up into the air. Then the action started.

Again we ran back and forth across the field. Again the towa sailed through the air over and over. And again I felt an excitement I hadn't experienced doing anything else in my short life.

Two and a half hours zipped by in the blink of an eye. Our team managed to win this time, by two points. As before, the two teams got together to drink some water and talk about the game.

James and I had a couple of friendly jabs back and forth. Then Charley came over to speak to me.

"Good game, Randy," he said.

"Thanks," I responded. I finished one last gulp of water. "I need to talk to you," I added.

"Sure, what about?"

"High school team sports," I said.

"Okay," Charley said. "Give me a minute to wrap things up with the team. Then we'll talk."

After Charley said good-bye to the other team members and gathered up his stickball gear, he came back to me. We walked toward the front of the community center where his car was parked.

"What's going on?" Charley asked.

"My dad and older brother were these great sports heroes," I began. "Baseball and football were their sports. Now the school principal and the coach expect me to follow in their footsteps. They expect me to help them win a state championship."

"Your older brother was the one killed in Iraq, wasn't he?" Charley asked.

"Yeah," I said. "That was him. My father has always pushed me to be like him. To be a football star or something."

"And you aren't comfortable with that," Charley guessed. "You have your own ideas about what you want to do. Is that it?

"Exactly. How did you know?"

"Because I've been there," Charley said. "I had to deal with that sort of thing when I was younger."

"The problem is," I continued. "I've never been any good at sports. So it's a total surprise that I can play stickball. And I don't even know why I'm good at it. But I really like it."

"And they don't offer it at Choctaw Central High School," Charley said.

"Right. Next week Mr. Gilroy expects me to pick one of the team sports they have. All I want to do is play toli."

We reached the parking lot and stood near Charley's car. My mom pulled into the parking lot and headed over to where we were standing.

"I understand the kind of pressure you're feeling," Charley said. "I wasn't going to say anything yet, but I do have an offer for you."

"What's that?" I asked.

"In January, my team will begin regular practices to get ready for the World Series of Stickball at next summer's Choctaw Fair. I'm short a player for that team. I think you could fill that spot."

"Are you kidding me right now? It wouldn't be nice to tease me about this."

"I'm dead serious, Randy. Of course, you need to improve your skills and build up your strength. But you've got all the makings of a great toli player."

"That's awesome, but it still doesn't help me with my problem."

"We'll work on that together, all right?"

"Okay, thanks," I replied. My head was spinning a little. I couldn't believe I was actually wanted on a team. I was always the one who was picked last in gym.

I got into the car with Mom. On the ride home I told Mom what had just happened and asked for her help.

"I don't think now would be a good time to talk to your dad about this," Mom said. "He just saw the doctor and got some medicine. It will take some time for him to start getting better."

"What am I going to do in the meantime? I've got the principal and the coach pressuring me to pick a sport this coming week!"

"You could always choose one of their sports and start practicing," Mom said. "When they see how bad you are, maybe they'll realize you aren't like your dad or your brother."

"And Dad will have a fit when he finds out," I answered. "I know he will. That's how he always deals with my failures."

"Let me think this through," she said.

Mom was quiet for a few minutes as we drove.

"I know that your dad will object to your playing stickball. First he'll say there's no protective gear. No kneepads or shoulder pads. Even I have a problem with that. But more importantly, he'll say it's not a modern sport. It's something left over from the old Indian ways. These things are not relevant to today's life."

"Why does that matter to him so much?" I asked. "What's wrong with the old ways?"

"The answer to that is kind of long," Mom responded. "It might be best to hear it from him."

I looked out the window for a while as we drove. The hills and trees of the countryside whizzed by. Something in my mind shifted at that moment. I decided I'd had enough.

"Okay, you know what?" I said. "I'm sixteen and I'm tired of people expecting me to be something or someone I'm not. When Dad gets home from work, I'm going to tell him how it is."

"Good luck with that," Mom said as we turned into our neighborhood.

Chapter 7
No Way

For dinner that night Mom fixed Dad's favorite foods. We had fried catfish, black-eyed peas, okra, and cornbread. She even made a pecan pie. It all tasted great.

I knew she was trying to put him in a good mood. That way it might be easier for him to hear what I needed to tell him.

Dad finished his last bite of pie. Mom poured him a cup of coffee.

"Ned, Randy needs to tell you something," Mom said to Dad as she put the coffee pot down. "And I want you to listen to him. It's important to him." She sat down at the table.

Dad wiped pie from the corner of his mouth and sipped the coffee. He waited. My stomach tightened.

"Dad, I don't want to play football or baseball," I blurted out.

"Oh, what do you want to play?" he asked. "Basketball? I hope it's not soccer. That's not even a real American sport."

"Stickball," I said.

"Say what?" Dad replied. He almost spit out a mouthful of coffee.

"Stickball. Toli."

"You mean running around in your shorts behind the community center on Saturdays? That's not a real sport."

"Actually it *is* a real sport, and I'm talking about playing on a team that will compete at the Choctaw Fair next summer."

Dad slammed his fist down on the table. The plates and glasses shook. I almost jumped out of my seat. He stood up.

"Now see here, boy," Dad boomed down at me. "I won't hear of it. That's not who we are as Choctaws any more. And it won't help you get into college anywhere."

"Ned, calm down," Mom interrupted. "You know the doctor said not to get excited."

"Stay out of it, woman," he demanded. "This is between the boy and me." He looked hard at her. Mom began clearing the dishes from the table.

"Stickball and those other things are part of the past," Dad said. "They need to stay in the past where they belong. We're Americans and we play American sports."

"But I'm not any good at those sports," I explained. "There are plenty of Choctaws who still do the old things. They play stickball, make Indian crafts, and hold traditional dances."

"And they'll never amount to anything important," he argued. "They're quaint relics from bygone days."

"Ned, you need to tell Randy why you believe that," Mom said, putting a stack of dirty dishes in the sink. "He has a right to know why you think that way. All you do is bark at him!"

Just then a ringing came from the kitchen counter. The sound startled my dad. Mom quickly turned it off. She had set a timer to go off when it was time for Dad to take his medicine.

I think the ringing made Dad lose track of what he was saying. Or maybe it was because he got upset. He took a deep breath and looked around. It was like he suddenly realized where he was or what he was doing. He sat down.

Mom handed him a pill and a glass of water. He took the pill and drank the water. Then he looked back at me. His face seemed softer. His eyes weren't as angry.

"Times change," he said in a calm voice. "People change. After World War II, in the 1940s, Indians all over the country were ready to begin living a modern life. To be like other Americans. The old ways seemed outdated."

Dad stopped talking and rubbed the side of his head like it hurt.

"Maybe you should go lie down," Mom said to him.

"I will in a minute," he replied. "Let me finish this first." He turned back to me.

"My father and grandfather tried to hold on to the old ways," he continued. "They were stubborn men. They didn't want those things to die out. But when I got to be a teenager, I didn't want anything to do with the old ways."

"So you played baseball?" I asked.

"That's right," Dad answered. "And it didn't come easy. I practiced hours every day so I'd get good at it. And my mother supported me in this all the way. She and I thought a lot alike."

I looked at my mother. I was thankful she was trying to support me in my decision.

Dad closed his eyes and wrinkled up his forehead. He looked tired.

"Okay, that's enough for now," Mom said. "Time to rest." Dad seemed too worn out to object. Maybe the medicine was doing that. I wasn't sure. Mom got him up and headed him out of the kitchen.

"No stickball—no way," he called out as he shuffled down the hall. "End of discussion."

When my mother came back into the kitchen she said, "That didn't go well, did it?"

"It was terrible," I said. "What am I going to do now?"

"I have an idea we could try," Mom offered. "Want to hear it?"

"Of course," I said. Hope was still alive, I thought.

"Next week I'll set up a meeting with your principal. I'll tell him I'm concerned about your grades. I'll tell him I don't want you spending time after school at sports practice. I want you to focus on schoolwork during your first year at high school."

"Okay, I'm with you so far."

"Now I wouldn't normally suggest this," Mom continued almost in a whisper. "It's a bit of a lie." She peeked down the hall to make sure the coast was clear. "I think you should continue playing stickball on Saturdays," she said.

"Really? What about Dad?"

"I can tell Dad that the school wants you to focus on your schoolwork this year," Mom said. "That they think you should hold off on playing any sports until your grades are better."

"So we can blame each of them for me not playing a school sport. Sounds risky. Think it'll work?" I asked.

"Maybe, but there's a catch," Mom said. "I *am* concerned about your grades. You *do* need to focus on schoolwork. So here's the deal. I'm willing to set this up for you as long as you promise to study harder and make better grades."

"But I'm already doing the best I can," I said.

"No, you're not," Mom replied. "I know you can do better."

"If you say so," I finally said. "But I need some help with schoolwork."

"The tribe has afternoon homework help at the community center. You'll spend every school-day afternoon there until your grades are up."

"And I can play stickball?"

"And you can play stickball, at least for now," Mom confirmed. We shook hands on the deal.

So for the rest of the fall semester I went to tutoring sessions at the community center after school. They helped me work on the subjects I was having trouble with. Math was at the top of the list, followed by science and reading. Did I leave anything out?

I decided to tell Jennifer I didn't have time to be anyone's boyfriend right now. I said I had too much on my plate. She took it hard for about five minutes. I guess she realized there was other boyfriend material out there. I kept on riding to and from school with her and her mother. But from then on I always sat in the back seat by myself.

On Saturdays I played stickball with Charley and the others. That put me at the community center six days a week. They got to know me pretty well around there.

But I think I got to be known a little *too* well.

A few days before Christmas, my family went to the yearly Christmas dinner held there. The gathering room was decked out with decorations made by Choctaw kids. The Christmas tree was covered with ornaments created from all natural things. There were pinecones hanging from red ribbons and leaves that had been spray-painted gold. Strings of colored popcorn circled the branches.

After we finished eating, Santa Claus came into the room. He was immediately surrounded by a swarm of children. They all needed to tell him what they wanted for Christmas.

"Ho, ho, ho," he said in a booming voice. "You children line up over there in the corner by the Christmas tree. You can tell Santa what you want for Christmas. But only if you've been good all year." He laughed another loud laugh. The children all ran for the tree. Santa gathered up his big red bag.

That Santa Claus looked a little familiar to me. So I got close enough to see who was underneath the beard and costume. It turned out to be Mr. Tubby. He had some additional padding around the middle to help him fill out the Santa suit.

We talked for a couple of minutes. Then Dad came over to tell me it was time to leave. It was then that Santa, Mr. Tubby, spoke to my dad. Too bad for me.

"Ned Cheska, it's been awhile," Mr. Tubby said. "Randy must be your son." His voice sounded a bit odd. It seemed like he was being polite, but not really friendly.

Dad looked closer at the man behind the beard. He stiffened a little. It seemed as though these two men knew each other but maybe didn't like each other too much.

"Carl Tubby," Dad said. "I didn't recognize you in the outfit. I thought you moved away from here."

"I'm back. Been back awhile. Please excuse me. I've got to go play Santa. See you around." He picked up his bag of toys. Before he left he shook my hand.

"See you Saturday as usual, Randy," he said. "I'm really impressed with your improved toli skills." He smiled and headed for the kids in the corner.

Uh-oh, I thought. The cat's out of the bag. The beans have been spilled.

My father's brown face turned bright red. His eyes burned angry.

"What did he mean by that, Randy?" he asked. "He'll see you Saturday as usual. Your toli skills have improved. What's he talking about?"

Dad asked these questions as though he already knew the answers. And he didn't like those answers.

"He's been playing stickball every Saturday," Mom's voice said from behind us. I looked over to see her just as she walked up to us.

"I told him he could," she added. "It's what he wants to do."

Dad looked like he was about to explode. But he didn't. Instead his eyes rolled back in his head. Then he fell to the floor.

Chapter 8
Old Ways/New Ways

Mom and I followed the ambulance that took Dad to the Neshoba County Hospital over thirty miles away. We sat together in the waiting room while the doctors examined him.

"What could've happened?" I wondered. "Did I make Dad so angry he had a heart attack?" I was worried and felt a bit guilty too, like this was somehow my fault. Mom was almost frantic.

In a little while a doctor came out and spoke to us. He said Dad had a tumor pressing on his brain. That sounded way beyond serious. The good news was that it wasn't cancer. They could operate on him in the morning. He should be able to go home within a few days, the doctor said.

Mom called my Aunt Issi who lived north of us about twenty miles. She came to the hospital, picked me up, and took me home to my house. She stayed with me while Mom sort of camped out at the hospital to be near Dad.

Aunt Issi was my dad's sister, but I didn't see her much. It seemed that there was some old argument between her and Dad. They didn't talk to each other. I never really knew what it was about. I thought now was as good a time as any to find out.

"Aunt Issi, how come you and Dad don't get along?" I asked when we got home.

"He never told you?" she asked me back.

"No," I said. "I'm just now starting to hear a few things about how he grew up. About how he didn't want to follow the old Choctaw ways."

"That's the very thing that separated us," she said. "The old ways against the new ways. Many Indians came to believe you couldn't do both. Your father was one of them. But, like your grandfather, I believed you could."

"Sounds possible to me," I offered.

"You would've had to grow up when we did to understand. It was different back then. The churches and the schools were teaching us that we couldn't follow the old Indian ways. They tried to make us believe that those ways were somehow bad. We were supposed to be like our white American neighbors. But things have changed since then, and I'm glad."

"Dad hasn't changed," I said with a sigh and a yawn.

"Time for bed," Issi said. "We'll talk more in the morning."

I started to head for my room, then stopped. "I've always wanted to know. What does your name, Issi, mean?" I asked.

"It means 'deer' in Choctaw," she answered. "My name is Deer. Did you know your father's name is really Neshoba, not Ned?"

"No! What does Neshoba mean?"

"It means 'wolf.' Your grandfather named all four of his kids for animals. Your other aunt and uncle who live in Alabama are named Nita and Fala. That's 'bear' and 'crow' in our language."

"Deer, Bear, Crow and Wolf," I said. "Cool names."

"Yeah, way cool," Issi agreed. "Now off to bed with you. Tomorrow we'll drive back to the hospital."

Off to bed I went. As I lay there I thought about what animal name I'd choose if I could. Maybe Bobcat or Badger. How about Cougar? I drifted off to sleep before deciding.

It was Christmas break so I didn't have to worry about school for a while. A few days passed as we waited to hear about Dad's condition. The doctor said the operation went well and everything would be fine.

Several days after the operation, I was allowed to go into Dad's room where he was recovering. He was sitting up in bed. A bandage was wrapped around his head. Mom was standing beside the bed. I stood across the room.

"Hey, Randy," Dad said as I got closer.

"Hey, Dad," I said. "How are you feeling?"

"Very glad to be alive," he said softly. "Because there's something I need to tell you. Please come closer."

I took a few steps toward the bed.

"I'm very sorry for the way I've been treating you," he said. His eyes got watery. "They told me they'd have to operate to remove this brain tumor. And the only thing I could think of was this. What if I died without telling my son that I loved him and wanted him to be happy?"

I didn't expect to hear that at all. I took the few remaining steps to the bed. I leaned over and hugged my father. Even though he had been hard on me, I still loved him.

"And then I had another thought," he continued. "What if I survived the surgery and didn't allow my son to be who he was or do what was important to him?"

I looked up into my dad's eyes. "What are you saying, Dad?" I asked.

"Your mother told me how good you were at playing stickball," he said. "How the team captain had asked you to play on his team. She said that playing toli would give you a chance to build your confidence. It would allow you to follow in Jack's footsteps in your own way."

He looked over at Mom. She took his hand in hers.

"Your mother is a smart lady," he said with a smile. "And I'm a stubborn mule." All three of us hugged. Dad even hugged Aunt Issi and told her he was sorry. I figured we'd be seeing more of her from now on.

Dad was able to come home from the hospital just after Christmas. When school started again after the winter break, I was ready to start practicing serious stickball.

That's when I got my next surprise. Charley set the practice schedule for Saturday afternoons at the usual place. I arrived at my first practice to find a field full of adults. I must've gotten the time wrong, I thought.

"Randy, I'm glad you could make it," Charley called from across the field. He jogged over to me.

"There must be some mistake," I said. "Did I miss my team's practice?"

"What do you mean? This *is* your team," he said. "I thought you understood that this was the men's team you'd be playing on. Only men's teams can play in the Choctaw stickball championship games."

Some of the men moved closer to hear the conversation.

"Charley said you're the best natural-born stickball player he's seen," one of the men said. "Welcome to the team." He held out his hand for me to shake.

I was in shock. I was overwhelmed. I didn't move. The man reached out and grabbed my arm. He took my hand in his and shook it. The other men lined up to shake my hand too. I counted each hand that I shook. There were twenty-nine. Men of all ages.

"I'm a lot smaller than you guys," I said. "I'll get creamed out there."

"This team will protect you," Charley said. "They've all sworn an oath to block, smash, or flatten any player on any other team who even thinks about roughing you up."

And that was that.

The practices began, along with my unbelievable career on the men's Oka Homma stickball team. The name Oka Homma means "Red Water" in Choctaw.

Of course, I had to still go to tutoring sessions after school to keep my grades up. Mom checked on my grades often. So I had to pay attention in class and pay attention in tutoring. That's the price I had to pay for playing stickball.

A couple of evenings a week and every Saturday I was out on the field. When it was too cold or rainy, we'd use the nearby Red Water Elementary School gym to exercise and practice our plays.

I found that good stickball teams ran plays like football teams do. You have to have a plan for getting the towa down the field and to the goal. Otherwise the game was just chaos.

That's what it looked like to people on the sidelines. The game didn't seem organized at all. But it really was.

Dad went back to his job at Fall-Mart, but he seemed like a new man. He was less angry and more friendly. Mom said the tumor had been part of his problem before. But most of Dad's troubles in life came because he had been so stubborn.

"The doctor must've removed the stubbornness right along with the tumor," she laughed. "I'd forgotten how much fun your dad used to be."

He even showed up at my stickball practices from time to time, and a few of our Saturday practice games when he didn't have to work.

Things were going so well I got up the courage one evening at dinner to tell Mom and Dad about the dream I'd had about Jack.

"I was afraid to tell you about it," I said. "I was afraid you'd think I was crazy. Or that I was just trying to make you think— Actually, I don't know what I thought would happen."

When I finished talking, my dad was silent for a couple of minutes. He was hardly breathing, and a tear formed in the corner of one eye. He wiped it with his napkin.

"I totally forgot about it until now," Dad said, "but I had a dream about Jack at around the same time. I didn't want to tell anyone about it either."

I couldn't believe it.

"In my dream, Jack was in his football uniform," Dad continued. "He said it was time for me to let go of him. Otherwise, he couldn't move on. He also said if I kept trying to control things and people, like Randy, I might make myself sick."

Mom and I sat in silence. "Wow," I thought. "It was more than just a dream. It really was Jack somehow reaching out to us. He was trying to help us from the other side."

The following Sunday our family attended the nearby Memorial Methodist Church for the first time in a long time. We wanted to let Jack know that his spirit had touched us. The preacher was glad to see us and invited us to come back real soon.

When Aunt Issi heard about our matching dreams, she called it "powerful medicine." She invited us to her house out in the country for a Choctaw ceremony. Dad wasn't so sure about it, but we went anyway.

An old Choctaw medicine man did a ceremony for us. He said it was to bless us because a departed family member had visited us from the spirit world. He said it would also keep us safe from having any unwanted spirit visitors coming to see us.

He sang a Choctaw song and had us drink a bitter-tasting tea he'd made. He prayed a long time in the Choctaw language. Then we all went inside and had a feast. That was the best part.

After that we went back to our regular lives. I really didn't know what to make of it all. Or which one to believe in—church preachers or Indian doctors. But I thought it was better to cover all the bases.

Chapter 9
Fair Play

On the last day of school, Principal Gilroy called me into his office. Coach Boles was there too. They were looking at my report cards for the year.

"It looks like you managed to improve your grades this year," Mr. Gilroy said. "Your parents must be pleased. And I guess that means you'll be able to get involved in sports here at the high school next year."

"I guess you didn't hear," I said. "I'm on a men's stickball team. I'm playing toli now. That's my sport. We play with no pads, no helmets, and no cleats. Football is for wimps!"

The two men just looked at each other in disbelief.

"You should consider adding stickball to the school's list of sports," I continued. "I think toli is the national sport of the Mississippi Choctaw Nation. This *is* the *Choctaw* Central High School, after all."

The principal and the coach were very disappointed. They almost reminded me of a couple of teenagers who didn't get their way. Mr. Gilroy dismissed me from his office just as the final school bell rang. I was glad to be out of there. On to summer!

The month of June was filled with stickball practices. Of course, most of the men had day jobs so we practiced at night. That was better anyway.

People said summers in Mississippi were so hot you could fry an egg on the sidewalk. I didn't know if that was true, but it was hot. And humid. So humid you could cut the air with a knife. That's the other thing people said about Mississippi.

At the beginning of July, Charley got the game schedule for the Choctaw Fair tournament known as the World Series of Stickball. He showed me this year's list of teams. Twelve Choctaw communities would be competing for the championship.

The Choctaw Fair took place in the middle of July each year. The first set of tournament games would be held the weekend before. The finals would take place during the fair. All games were played on the Choctaw Central High School football field.

In our first match, we'd face a team called Tushka Homma, which means "Red Warrior." So it would be Red Water against Red Warrior.

Game time arrived Saturday at eight p.m. The games were held at night for the same reason our practices were held at night. Heat and humidity.

Mom and Aunt Issi came to the stadium to watch and cheer on our team. Dad had to work the late shift at the store. That was disappointing, but no big deal. There would be other games.

I walked onto the field with my teammates. We were all wearing our brand-new uniforms. Red T-shirts and black gym shorts. Each player had a number printed on the front and back. Above the number was our team name: Oka Homma.

The large electric scoreboard at the end of the field was lit up and ready to go. It was usually used for the high school's football games. Now it would mark off four quarters for stickball and keep track of our scores.

Mom called to me from the stands and I waved. Only a few spectators were on hand to watch. This wasn't as important a game as the ones during the Choctaw Fair.

Then all the Oka Homma players gathered in a tight bunch on our side of the field. We held our sticks above our heads.

"Who are we?" Charley called from the middle of the group.

"Oka Homma!" we all called back.

"Who's gonna win this game?" Charley asked loudly.

"Oka Homma!" we screamed as loud as we could.

Then we rattled our sticks together. The clack, clack, clack of the sticks rang out across the field.

We were pumped up and ready to play! As the youngest and smallest player, I knew I wouldn't be playing during much of our first game. Charley needed the strongest and fastest players out there. I was backup.

Only ten of our thirty players were out on the field at any one time. The rest watched from the sidelines and waited their turn. But no one waited long. Running up and down the field was tiring. So Charley substituted players often. That kept the players fresh.

A referee blew the whistle and the game began! Our opponents played hard and fast. The towa moved quickly back and forth across the field. Our team scored, and then the other team scored. By halftime we were tied four to four.

Charley let me play a few times during the second half. I was grateful. I held my own ground and didn't embarrass the team once.

We squeaked by to win our first tournament game by one point, nine to eight! What a rush! I was exhausted and exhilarated at the same time.

After the game, Charley pulled us all together. "Great game, guys!" he said. "Now we move on to the next round. The schedule says we'll be playing again this Thursday night at eight o'clock. We'll do one more practice at the community center Tuesday night to get ready. See you then."

At home I found out Dad had to work the late shift again Thursday night. He wouldn't see that game either.

"Are you ever going to take time off to watch me play?" I asked him.

"I don't have control over my work schedule, son," He answered. "I'll try to get off Thursday night. But if you make it to the championship game Saturday night, I'll call in sick if I have to. I'll be there."

Dad couldn't get off work Thursday night after all. But Mom and Aunt Issi were there. It was great to have some of my family there to cheer for us. A lot more people showed up to watch this one. Jennifer and her new boyfriend even showed up.

This time we were up against a team called the War Hawks. They had a reputation for playing dirty. Charley was a little worried.

Things went badly for us the first half of the game. At halftime we were down by three points. Two of our best players were hurt and couldn't play.

"This team is a lot tougher than I thought," Charley said at our halftime huddle. "We need to use a different strategy with them."

He checked a clipboard where he kept play notes. Then he smiled.

"Let's try the old fake-out play until we catch up," he said. "Randy, remind us how that goes."

"Well, we use this play when the ball is on the ground and we're circling it with our sticks," I said. "If one of our players gets hold of the ball, the next player to the right of him pretends he got the ball too. Both players clasp their sticks together like they have the towa."

"That's right," Charley said. "Keep going."

"Both players run toward the goal like they're going to score," I continued. "A few of the other team's players will go after each of our players. Their attention will be split. The other team will eventually figure out who really has the ball. But for a little while they won't know for sure. It could give us enough time to move past them to score."

"Very good," Charley said. "Now let's go win this thing!"

We put our sticks up together in the middle of the team cluster and screamed "Oka Homma" as loud as we could.

The fake-out play worked just well enough for us to catch up with the War Hawks. By the beginning of the last quarter we were tied eight to eight. The score didn't change until there were only two minutes left in the game.

Charley decided to use the fake-out play one more time to see if we could break the tie. He told me to try to get into position to be the one to fake it. When our fastest runner grasped the ball between his sticks, I was just to the right of him. We both turned away from the cluster. Then we both headed toward the other team's goalpost.

But a War Hawk player decided it was time to pull one of the dirty plays they were famous for. He ran up beside me and used his sticks to trip me. I went flying sideways for a split second. Then I hit the ground. Hard. One shoulder and one knee skidded across the grass.

As I lay on the ground in pain, I watched as my brother player scored the point just before the final buzzer sounded. We won! We'd be playing in the championship game!

Charley ran over to help me get up. Right behind him were my mother and aunt. They must've run like lightning to get from the stands so fast.

"I'm all right," I said as I stood up. I looked down at my knee. It was bloody and scraped. My shoulder wasn't as bad.

"We need to get that looked at immediately," Mom said with a worried tone of voice. She took me by the arm. "I think that's enough stickball for a while."

I pulled away from her.

"I don't care if I'm on crutches," I blurted out. "I'm not going to miss the championship game. I've worked too hard."

I hobbled off toward the sidelines where I knew Charley kept a first aid kit. Charley followed. My shoulder and knee hurt a lot, but I wasn't going to let it show.

Aunt Issi pulled my mother aside and said something to her. I couldn't hear what she said, but I'm pretty sure she was helping to make my case.

"Randy, you're a minor," Charley said. "If one of your parents says you can't play, then I have to do what they say. It's going to be up to you to get your mom to agree."

This was just great, I thought. First Dad didn't want me to play. Now my mother was the problem. What was I going to do?

Chapter 10
The Challenge

When we got home, Dad was there. I'd have to convince him to somehow override Mom on this. I laid out my case to Dad like a lawyer talking to a judge. I hoped he would be on my side since he'd played sports.

He and Mom went into the kitchen while I got cleaned up and ready for bed. Their voices got louder and louder until all went quiet. Finally Dad came into my room.

"Your mother is going to let you play," he said. Boy, was I relieved.

"On one condition," he continued.

"What?" I asked.

"You have to win the championship!" Dad smiled real big.

"Woo-hoo!" I hollered.

"And have those wounds bandaged all through the game," he added as he pointed his finger at me. "Both your mother and I will be there to make sure everything is going smoothly. If you get hurt again, we'll pull you out immediately. Got that?"

"Got it," I said. "Thanks, Dad. This really means a lot."

Dad and I talked some more about the game we'd just won and about stickball in general. I couldn't think of a time when we had connected so well.

Saturday came. My uniform had been washed. My cuts and scrapes were tightly bandaged. We drove to the stickball field at around six o'clock. We wanted to get some Choctaw food at the fair and see some of the other activities there.

Charley wanted us on the field an hour early so we could get psyched up for the game. At nine o'clock I walked on the field carrying my sticks. The rest of the team was gathering.

To my surprise, Mr. Gilroy and Coach Boles were there talking to Charley. The two men turned toward me as I approached.

"These two gentlemen have something to tell you," said Charley.

"Randy, I am so impressed with your performance on this team," Principal Gilroy said. "Coach Boles and I have been giving serious thought to your suggestion about teaching stickball at the high school."

"That's awesome," I said."

"We have to present the idea to the school board and get their approval," Coach Boles added. "But we wanted you to know that we heard you. Good luck with tonight's game. We'll be watching from the stands."

They headed for their seats. My team headed for a huddle.

"We've made it to the championship game," Charley said. "I'm proud of all of you, no matter how this game ends."

Out of the corner of my eye I saw a half dozen people headed toward us. They were dressed in traditional Choctaw clothes. One of the men carried a drum.

"To help us get prepared tonight," Charley said, "I've asked some traditional Choctaw singers to put us in a Choctaw state of mind. They'll sing a couple of songs for us. And while we're playing on the field, they'll stay on the sidelines to give us strength."

The singers stepped in close to us and began their songs. I didn't know what the words meant, but they sounded good. The music felt good too.

"As they sing, I'd like to give any of you guys a chance to say a few words about what you're feeling. That is, if you want to."

Charley stepped back to see if anyone on the team would come forward. Chester, one of the players, stepped up.

"I've felt a stronger connection to stickball than to any other sport I've ever tried," he said.

"Wow," I thought. "He took the words right out of my mouth."

"Stickball is part of who we are," he continued. "It's part of our tribal identity. I'm glad I'm playing with you guys. Oka Homma!"

Everyone shouted in unison, "Oka Homma!"

Finally I decided to speak. "I've come to realize that playing stickball is more than just a game. It's like . . . it makes me want to learn more about my culture. It makes me want to learn more about who I am."

The other players nodded their heads in agreement.

The singing ended. We had to switch gears. Time to man up! We did our warm-up exercises to loosen up.

By game time the stands were full of people. There must've been five hundred people there. Maybe more. I scanned the crowd until I found Dad, Mom, and Aunt Issi. I waved to them happily. Then I noticed Jennifer and her mother sitting nearby. No boyfriend this time. Jennifer waved sweetly. I gave her a quick wave before turning back to the field.

To win this year's World Series of Stickball we had to beat a team called Tushka Neshoba. Wolf Warriors. They were famous far and wide in the world of stickball. They were also last year's champions. We had our work cut out for us.

As the game began, Charley told me he was saving me for the second half. He said I was his secret weapon. I knew he was just saying that so I wouldn't feel bad. He was really worried about me getting hurt some more. And worried about what my parents would say if I did.

At the end of the first half we were down by two points. The score was five to three, a low-scoring game for us. Our defense had prevented Tushka Neshoba from scoring several times. All were close calls. But the other team's defense had also prevented us from making several points. They were worthy opponents. It was hard staying on the sidelines when all I wanted was to be out there in the thick of it.

Surprisingly, Charley really did put me in when the second half began.

"I want to use your smaller size to our advantage," he said. "It's time to razzle-dazzle them with the play you've been practicing."

"Absolutely!" I responded with great enthusiasm.

"This may be hard to pull off because of your injuries," Charley offered. "Are you sure you're up to it?"

"I'll pull this off if it's the last thing I ever do," I said as I ran onto the field with the other players.

It was obvious to the Tushka Neshoba players that I was injured. My bandages announced that fact loud and clear. A few of them tried to take advantage of that by attempting to hit me on those very spots. But Chester and the others on my team were right there. After a few well-placed, painful tackles, the other team laid off me.

Then it came my time to perform. There was a thick cluster of players circling the ball on the ground. Our sticks clattered together as each of us tried in vain to capture the towa.

My smaller size allowed me to squeeze in between the larger players.

Finally I grabbed the ball between the two nets of my sticks. But instead of turning to run with the ball, I simply rolled backward away from the cluster of players. As my back hit the ground I flung the ball through the air toward the other team's goalpost. One of our players had been standing by. He caught the ball with his sticks. Immediately he flipped the ball to an Oka Homma player waiting near the goal. He caught it and hit the post. The play happened so fast that the opposing players hardly knew what hit them.

Our supporters in the crowd went wild. They were screaming "Oka Homma! Oka Homma!" over and over.

That play was just enough to throw the other team off guard a little. So during the next play of the ball, we pulled the old fake-out routine. To my surprise, that worked, too. The score was all tied up, five to five.

Charley called me to the sidelines and put someone else in for me. When I reached the area where he was standing, he pointed to my bandages. Both had been torn loose. My injuries had started to bleed a little.

"You've done your part tonight," he said. "You get to watch the rest of the game from here."

"But—!"

"No buts about it," Charley said. "Remember our deal. Now get those injuries taken care of."

I knew he was right. I got fresh bandages and put them on. I stayed on the sidelines and watched our team play the rest of the game. Mom, Dad, and Issi joined me during the last few minutes. It was great having them there. Miraculously, Oka Homma did win the game and the championship!

The families of all the players streamed onto the field to congratulate us. I stood in the line of Oka Homma's thirty players in the middle of the field. The opposing team moved down the line, shaking our hands. Then our team supporters moved down the line, and we shook their hands.

I was so happy we'd won. But at the same time, I was a little disappointed I wasn't on the playing field at the end. Dad said I had nothing to be down about. I was the smallest and youngest player on a proud winning team. And I had made a real contribution to the victory.

I knew Dad was right. I knew Charley had been right to take me out when he did. But I was still a little disappointed.

Chapter 11
Head to Head

I took it easy for a week or so after the game so my injuries could heal. The following Saturday, Charley paid me a surprise visit. He came into the living room and we sat down to talk. Mom said she'd make us some lemonade.

"This is for you," he said after Mom had left the room. He handed me a large envelope. I opened it. Inside was an eight-by-ten photo taken after we'd won the championship game. The entire team stood near the scoreboard. In front of us on the ground was the championship trophy.

"Thanks," I said. "This is great."

"I know you're still a little down because you didn't get to finish out the game," Charley said.

"I know I shouldn't be, but I am," I admitted.

"Well, maybe the news I have will cheer you up."

"Oh yeah. What news?" I asked.

"As the best Mississippi Choctaw stickball team, we've been challenged to an intertribal match with the Oklahoma Choctaws," he said.

"Really?" I asked. "I didn't know the Oklahoma Choctaws played stickball. Actually, I never really thought about it before."

"Our western cousins' culture has been coming back strong the past few years," Charley said. "Stickball is part of that revival." He paused as Mom brought us two glasses of lemonade. She went back to the kitchen.

"And here's another thing you might not know," he went on. "To some tribes, the ancient game of stickball was also known as the Little Brother of War."

"Little Brother of War? Why was it called that?" I asked.

"Because the game was sometimes played to settle conflicts between communities or tribes instead of going to war," Charley explained. "The game took the place of war. Those matches were played on huge fields, sometimes with hundreds of players. These were very rough, very serious events."

"Little Brother of War." I thought about it for a moment. "That's a more impressive name than stickball."

"So the best team among the Oklahoma Choctaws has invited us to their rez for the competition," Charley continued. "It'll be held Labor Day weekend as part of their annual festival. We'll play five games. The best three out of the five takes the title."

He pulled a letter out of his back pocket and handed it to me. "Here's a copy of the invitation letter with the dates and location," Charley said. "Talk to your parents and let me know. We need you for those games."

He finished his lemonade and stood to leave. Mom came in to say good-bye.

"I don't know where it came from," Charley said to Mom before heading out the door, "but stickball is in Randy's bloodline. One of his ancestors must've been a great player."

After he left, I gave Mom the invitation letter to read. She had already said she didn't know if she wanted me to play stickball anymore. She felt it was too easy to get seriously hurt. I knew I had to work on Dad. I hoped he'd be more agreeable to it. Things had really changed in the last few months!

That evening at dinner I showed the letter to Dad. I sat quietly as he read it out loud. Then I told Mom and Dad about stickball's other name, Little Brother of War.

"In my dream of Jack, he kept calling me 'little brother,'" I said. "He told me to find another path instead of war. Don't you see? This is that path!"

It took another hour of pleading, whining, and convincing, but I finally wore them down. They said I could go to Oklahoma! I was way beyond excited! This would be my first trip without my parents!

I spent the month of August getting ready for the trip and the upcoming game. Mom helped me gather the camping gear I'd need. We'd be staying at the campground near their old tribal headquarters in the town of Tushkahoma, Oklahoma. Wait. I recognized those words. They were both Choctaw words!

On the Thursday before the Labor Day weekend, the team headed out. We had three full-sized vans filled with players and our gear. Only twenty of our players could go because some of them had to work or take care of family.

The 550-mile trip took about twelve hours with stops for gas and food. We arrived at the campground the same night. The schedule called for us to play five games in three days. The first game would be Friday night and the final game would be Sunday night. That would give us time to drive back home on Monday, which was the Labor Day holiday.

Friday afternoon was the opening of their annual Choctaw Nation Labor Day Festival. Our team was introduced to the crowd that had gathered. Everyone was very nice and welcoming. It was our first chance to see the other team. They didn't look so tough. They even had a kid on their team who looked to be about my age.

It wasn't until late that afternoon that our "secret weapon" arrived from back home. A car carrying a Choctaw medicine man, drummer, and singer pulled into the campground. They'd come from Mississippi to support our team.

Charley had explained a little about traditional Choctaw stickball teams. He said they were always helped by this type of "supernatural" support. They would chant, drum, and sing from the sidelines. He figured it wouldn't hurt to have a little of this kind of help for this competition.

At seven o'clock we all went to the stickball field. It was a great field for stickball because it wasn't also used for football. Nothing but stickball was played there. It was a large field of smooth, mowed grass with goalposts at either end.

When the first game began, our sideline supporters started doing their thing. The singer sang Choctaw songs of encouragement. The medicine man spoke ancient Choctaw words to bring us power. The drummer beat his drum faster or slower depending on the speed of the game.

The Oklahoma Choctaws had their own team of sideline supporters doing the same thing on the other side of the field. It all made the event sort of unreal. Or maybe it was very real, for a hundred years ago!

We lost the first game by three points. That was kind of a shock. We weren't worried about it, though. We were playing on their turf with their referees. They had the upper hand. The first game was a learning experience. Back at camp after the game we discussed what we'd learned about our opponents.

Our sideline support team said their supporters had cursed our side of the field before the game. That's what made us lose, they said. Of course, I had no experience with this kind of thing. It sounded a little wild to me.

The medicine man suggested we ask to change sides of the field. That should make a big difference. He said he and his support team would have to give it all they had. Tomorrow's two games would go better for sure, he told us. I crossed my fingers.

Saturday's first game started at two o'clock in the afternoon. The sun was shining and the wind was calm. The two stickball teams began their fight on the field. The two support teams also began their unseen fight.

Suddenly a wind came up from the east, blowing across the field into the faces of the Mississippi players. Then a competing wind came out of the west. It blew into the faces of the Oklahoma players.

The two winds collided in the middle of the field. A whirlwind of dust was stirred up and began making circles on the field. The players stopped in their tracks to watch the strange event. I couldn't believe what I was seeing.

The players of each team backed toward their own side of the field. We all wanted to give whatever it was plenty of room.

The whirlwind first twisted one way, then the other. It looked like it was fighting with itself. Suddenly it exploded and disappeared. All was silent for a while. Nothing moved. "What just happened?" I wondered.

We were all pretty shaken up by the ordeal. Charley walked toward the center of the ball field. The other team's captain did too. They talked quietly for a few minutes. Then Charley came back to us.

"We've decided to send our sideline support teams home," he said. "Their powers are creating too much chaos. Frankly, I really hadn't taken it seriously until now."

Charley explained the situation to our medicine man. The old man nodded his head. He, the drummer, and the singer packed up their things. The Oklahoma group did the same. From that point on, we were on our own.

When the sun went down Saturday evening, the Oklahoma Choctaws had won two games and we'd won one. At least we knew they were beatable. And we knew we had to win both of Sunday's games.

That night I was surprised to see the other team's young player wander into our camp. He made his way over to my tent and introduced himself.

"My name's Mitchell Leonard," he said, shaking my hand. I told him who I was and where I lived. "How old are you?" he asked.

I answered, "Sixteen. I'll be in the eleventh grade."

"You're a good player," he said. "I'm really happy to meet you." Give me your address. I'll write you. Next year we want to come to your Choctaw Fair in July."

"That'd be great," I said. We exchanged addresses and phone numbers.

"I'd wish you luck in tomorrow's games, but I want to win," Mitchell said. Where had I heard that before?

"Same for me," I replied. We chatted for a minute or two. Then he put my address in his pocket and left.

I went to bed very early that night. A big day was coming. I couldn't let Mitchell's team win.

By noon on Sunday, storm clouds began gathering in the area. It looked like a thunderstorm was brewing.

"What happens if it rains?" I asked Charley.

"We'll be getting very wet," he said. "They don't cancel a stickball game because of rain."

That day we played two of the soggiest, sloppiest games anyone could ever imagine. We slipped and slid up and down the field. The carpet of smooth green grass was shredded. By the end of the first game, mud covered every inch of me.

We had to resort to colored armbands to tell the teams apart. Red for our team. White for theirs. It reminded me of my very first game at the Red Water Community Center.

Once again the experience was exhausting and exhilarating. I had such a great time. And yet I wanted so badly to be clean and dry.

At the end of the day, we had won a game and lost a game. That put the weekend results at three games for Oklahoma and two games for us. We'd never played in the rain. All that mud and water was hard to deal with. On the other hand, they played like it happened all the time.

"We'll beat 'em next year on our home turf," Charley promised. "For now, they've arranged for us to use the nearby high school locker room showers to get cleaned up. How does that sound?"

That sounded absolutely great to me. A shower and a sleeping bag were all I needed at that point.

During the drive home the next day, I had plenty of time to think about events of the past year.

"We may have lost this tournament," I told Charley. "But I'll never forget this experience. Thanks for letting me be a part of it."

"When you're an old man, you're going to have some great stories to tell your grandkids," he said.

"Whoa, that's too much for my sixteen-year-old mind to think about," I replied. So I didn't.

Chapter 12
Supernatural

Charley dropped me off at my house late Monday night. On the ride back from Oklahoma, I'd heard many tall tales about stickball games of the past. Each one was more unbelievable than the last.

And Mom and Dad almost couldn't believe that we'd played in the middle of a thunderstorm. But they believed it when I showed them the muddy rags that were once my uniform.

"Randy, I'm so proud of you," Dad said. It made me feel good to hear it. What a difference a year had made.

"Come into the kitchen," he said. "I want to show you something."

The three of us went into the kitchen. On the table sat a dusty cardboard box. Written on the side were the words "Gramps' Things."

"I found this up in the attic," Dad explained. "I'd forgotten all about it until yesterday. This was your grandfather's stuff. It's been up there since we moved into this house."

He opened the top flaps of the box. I looked inside. There was an old photo album, a small box, and something long wrapped in an old piece of leather. Dad took out the photo album and thumbed through it. When he found what he was looking for, he handed the album to me.

On the left page of the open album there was a faded old photograph. It was a black-and-white picture of a stickball team. A stickball team! Written on the bottom of the photo were the words "Choctaw Fair 1949."

"Wow, this is awesome," I said.

On the right page there was a yellowed newspaper article and a list of the names of the players. Dad pointed to one of the men in the photo.

"That is your great-grandfather," he said and then pointed to a name on the list. "And over here is his name, R. Jackson Cheska," he said. "His full name was Randall Jackson Cheska, but everyone called him RJ."

I blinked a couple of times. Did I hear him right?

"That's right," Dad said. "We named you and Jack after my grandfather."

"How come I never knew that?" I wondered.

Dad reached into the box one more time and came up with a small box. He handed it to me and I opened it. Inside was a small medallion attached to a ribbon.

"I think that was your great-grandfather's too," Dad said. "Look at the picture and you'll see they're all wearing one of these. Instead of a trophy, I think they all got one of these."

As I was looking at the photograph, I realized that one of the faces looked very familiar. I looked more closely. What a shock I got! There in the lineup was a man who looked a lot like Albert Isaac, the man who'd made my ball sticks. Actually, he looked *exactly* like Albert Isaac.

I looked at the list of names. And there it was in black and white: Albert Isaac.

"How is that possible?" I asked myself.

I explained to Mom and Dad what I'd found. And I retold the story of the old man in the community center who had disappeared.

Dad read a few lines of the faded newspaper article to himself.

"It says right here that Albert Isaac was their team coach and a ball stick maker," he said.

"How is that possible?" I asked myself a second time. My mind was reeling.

There was one more thing in the cardboard box. Something wrapped in worn leather. I was curious, so I picked it up.

Unwrapping the leather, I found a pair of well-used ball sticks inside. Though the wood was scarred and worn from use, the sticks were still in good enough condition to use. I turned them over and over in my hands. They were almost identical to the pair of kapoca I'd been using. The pair Albert Isaac had made.

I looked at the base of the sticks. To my great surprise, there was an *A* stamped on the bottom of one stick and an *I* on the other.

"How is that possible?" I asked myself yet a third time. I ran to the living room as fast as I could. In my duffle bag I found my own sticks. I took them back to the kitchen. Sitting side by side, the two sets of sticks were a perfect match. They could've been clones.

"Amazing," Mom said.

"Supernatural!" Dad said. "Gramps used to say the spirits of our Choctaw ancestors are with us still. I really never believed it before. I do now."

We were all quiet for a few minutes. I couldn't think. I was too overwhelmed. And tired. I stood up. As I did, I noticed there was one last thing in the cardboard box. It was a piece of paper. It looked like a page torn out of a book. It was yellowed and jagged on one edge. I picked it up.

Printed on the front side of the page was a book title: *The Social and Ceremonial Life of the Choctaw Indians*, by John Swanton, published 1931.

I flipped the page over. A handwritten message was on the other side. It read, "Today is the first day of the rest of your life."

I knew somehow Gramps had been with me the whole time. And Albert Isaac. I was grateful to them both. And in awe.

"Thanks, Gramps," I said. "Thanks, Albert."

The rest of my life could wait until tomorrow, I thought. I was tired and went to bed. As I was falling asleep I had a thought. We might have to start visiting the preacher *and* the medicine man on a regular basis. Just to cover all bases.

About the Author

Gary Robinson, a writer and filmmaker of Cherokee and Choctaw Indian descent, has spent more than twenty-five years working with American Indian communities to tell the historical and contemporary stories of Native people in all forms of media. His television work has aired on PBS, Turner Broadcasting, Ovation Network, and others. His nonfiction books, *From Warriors to Soldiers* and *The Language of Victory*, reveal little-known aspects of American Indian service in the U.S. military, from the Revolutionary War to modern times. He has also written two other novels, *Thunder on the Plains* and *Tribal Journey*, and two children's books that share aspects of Native American culture through popular holiday themes: *Native American Night Before Christmas* and *Native American Twelve Days of Christmas*. He lives in rural central California.

7th GENERATION

PathFinders novels offer exciting contemporary and historical stories featuring Native teens and written by Native authors.

For more information, visit:
NativeVoicesBooks.com

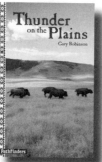

Thunder on the Plains
Gary Robinson
• 978-1-939053-00-8
• $9.95
• 128 pages

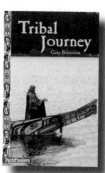

Tribal Journey
Gary Robinson
978-1-939053-01-5 •
$9.95 •
120 pages •

Danny Blackgoat, Navajo Prisoner
Tim Tingle
• 978-1-939053-03-9
• $9.95
• 160 pages

Available from your local bookstore or you can buy them directly from:

Book Publishing Company • P.O. Box 99 • Summertown, TN 38483
1-800-695-2241

Please include $3.95 per book for shipping and handling.